MONSTER HIGH™

TOO GHOUL FOR SCHOOL

SPECIAL THANKS TO
ERIC HARDIE

Stock photos: p. 1: Lim Chewltow/shutterstock.com (three-ring binder); p. 4: AKaiser/shutterstock.com (paper top); p. 4: Jill Battaglia/shutterstock.com (paper yellow); p. 4: ryabinina/shutterstock.com (paper bubble); p. 6: photka/shutterstock.com (paint swash); p. 6: Abel Tumik/shutterstock.com (lipstick); p. 6: ryabinina/shutterstock.com (scrap paper w/clip); p. 7: kuleczka/shutterstock.com (eyelashes); p. 7: kuleczka/shutterstock.com (nail polish/eyeshadow); p. 7: Picsfive/shutterstock.com (wrinkled paper); p. 8: c.byatt-norman/shutterstock.com (locker); p. 9: AKaiser/shutterstock.com (scrap paper); p. 11: Mazzzur/shutterstock.com (graph paper); p. 12: Picsfive/shutterstock.com (wrinkle paper); p. 12: BelkalO/shutterstock.com (yarn); p. 12: AKaiser/shutterstock.com (scrap paper); p. 14: Jenn Huls/shutterstock.com (yarn); p. 16: solita/istock.com (index card); p. 17: Sergiy Kuzmin/shutterstock.com (raspberries); p. 18: sai0112/shutterstock.com (strawberry); p. 18: hxdbzxy/shutterstock.com (chips); p. 19: ryabinina/shutterstock.com (paper text bubble); p. 21: Africa Studio/shutterstock.com (lab flask); p. 22: Mike Vande Ven Jr/shutterstock.com (rock candy); p. 27: Le Do/shutterstock.com (beachball); p. 27: LU HUANFENG/shutterstock.com (whistle); p. 28: Picsfive/shutterstock.com (paper); p. 28: Mega Pixel/shutterstock.com (clipboard); p. 28: KonstantinChristian/shutterstock.com (glasses); p. 29: stockphoto-graf/shutterstock.com (basketball); p. 29: Carolyn Franks/shutterstock.com (paper bag); p. 29: Jill Battaglia/shutterstock.com (lined torn paper); p. 31: Susan Schmitz/shutterstock.com (pom-poms); p. 31: Picsfive/shutterstock.com (lined pad of paper)

Cover design by Steve Scott
Interior design by Kay Petronio

Little, Brown and Company

Hachette Book Group
237 Park Avenue, New York, NY 10017
Visit our website at lb-kids.com

monsterhigh.com

Little, Brown and Company is a division of Hachette Book Group, Inc.
The Little, Brown name and logo are trademarks of Hachette Book Group, Inc.

The publisher is not responsible for websites (or their content)
that are not owned by the publisher.

First Edition: July 2014

Library of Congress Control Number: 2013952374

ISBN 978-0-316-27708-2

10 9 8 7 6 5 4 3 2 1

CW

Printed in the United States of America

TOO GHOUL FOR SCHOOL

A CREEPY-COOL ACTIVITY BOOK

WRITTEN BY POLLYGEIST DANESCARY

L B

LITTLE, BROWN AND COMPANY

NEW YORK BOSTON

ALMA MONSTER

As a new student at Monster High, it's important to learn the school's alma monster. We like to sing it after we win foot-ball and Casketball games—and we win a lot, so memorize the lyrics below, if you haven't already!

WE ARE MONSTER HIGH

We are monsters; we are proud.
We are monsters; say it loud.

High school's a horror, can't get out of my bed.
Everybody's talking, but it's not in my head.
They say, "Don't be different, be like them instead,"
But they can't keep us down 'cause we're Monster High–bred.

The clock is striking thirteen.
Whoa oh oh oh oh oh!
It's time to cheer for your team.
Whoa oh oh oh oh oh!
You are the ghoulest ghoul by far,
So don't be afraid of who you are.

'Cause tonight we're gonna leave our fears behind.
We're in it together!
Stepping out, and we're letting our spirits fly.
Stay fierce forever!
Wa wa wa wa-oh, freak out if you dare!
Wa wa wa wa-oh, your best nightmare!
Don't stop rocking your right to fright.
We are Monster High!

We are monsters; we are proud.
We are monsters; say it loud.
Come on!

Perfectly imperfect—and we do it our way.
United not divided—won't get cast away.
They say, "Go run and hide," but I just gotta say,
We're drop-dead gorgeous each and every day.

The clock is striking thirteen.
Whoa oh oh oh oh oh!
It's time to scream for your team.
Whoa oh oh oh oh oh!
We don't have to say good-bye,
'Cause friends like these will never die.

'Cause tonight we're gonna leave our fears behind.
We're in it together!
Come on, it's time to let our spirits fly.
Stay fierce forever!
Wa wa wa wa-oh, freak out if you dare!
Wa wa wa wa-oh, your best nightmare!
Don't stop rocking your right to fright.
We are Monster High!

We are monsters; we are proud.
We are monsters; say it loud.
We are Monster High!
We are monsters; we are proud.
We are monsters—we are Monster High!

Now gather your ghoulfriends together and scare up

the lyrics to your own alma monster. Take turns

writing one line at a time like Catty Noir, Operetta, and

Holt Hyde. You could also each write one entire

verse (four lines), then put your verses together!

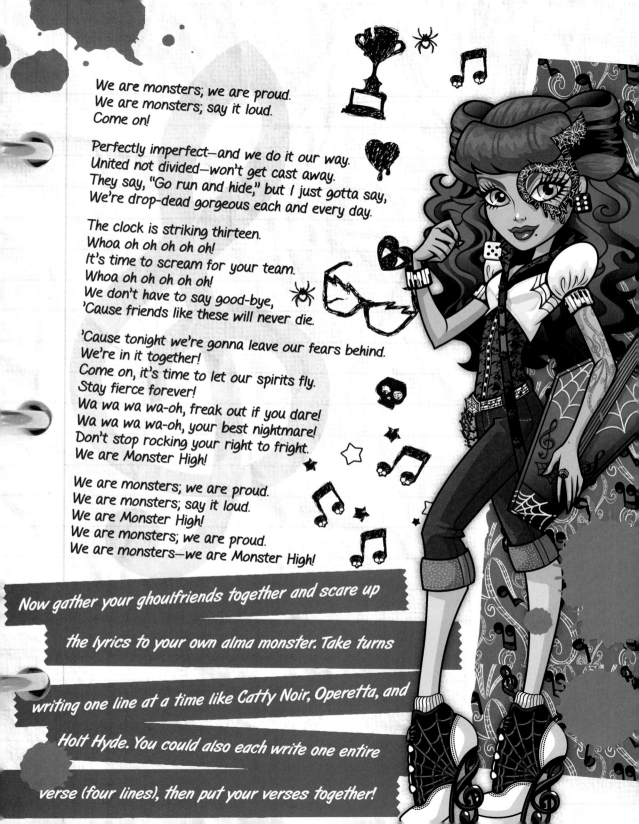

POLTERNALITY QUIZ

Which Monster High student are you most like? Take the quiz to find out!

1. How would you describe yourself?
a. adventurous
b. stylish
c. self-confident
d. fun-loving
e. responsible

2. What's your favorite thing to do with your ghoulfriends?
a. go to a scream park for a wild roller-coaster ride
b. shop for a super styling new haunt couture outfit at the Maul
c. have a frightfully fierce dance party
d. surf the waves at Gloom Beach
e. explore claw-some old buildings

3. What is your killer style?
a. anything with a watch so I won't be late
b. whatever is the latest trend
c. lots of ghoulgeous jewels
d. casual beachwear
e. something chic and sophisticated

4. Which class do you like beast?
a. Metal shop
b. Dragonomics
c. Dragonometry
d. Oceanography
e. Architecture

ROCK YOUR RIGHT TO FRIGHT

5. What is the beast way to cheer up one of your ghoulfriends?

a. go bungee jumping or rock climbing—the adrenaline rush will pep her up

b. give her a monstrous makeunder

c. just spend time with her—my creepy-cool company would make anyone happy

d. spend some time outside in the fresh air

e. remind her of all the claw-some things in her life

TURN THE PAGE TO CHECK YOUR RESULTS!

If you chose mostly **A**s, you're Robecca Steam, and you love wild adventure and excitement! Just try not to let the thrills make you lose track of time.

If you chose mostly **B**s, you're Clawdeen Wolf, and you're fangtastically fashionable! But do make some time to curl up with a good book every now and then. You want your mind to be just as on trend as the rest of you!

If you chose mostly **C**s, you're Cleo de Nile, and you are totally confident. Share the limelight you attract with your ghoulfriends to maximize the fun for everyone—including you!

If you chose mostly **D**s, you're Lagoona Blue, and you love to have fun in the sun. Bring the same enthusiasm you have for the outdoors inside with you to brighten your time in class!

If you chose mostly **E**s, you're Rochelle Goyle, and you're très responsighoul! Be sure to loosen up every so often and really go wild with your ghoulfriends.

COFFIN COOL

Draculaura's locker is plastered in hearts, Venus McFlytrap's locker has scary-cool recycled decorations, and Wydowna Spider's locker is decked out in skelegant cobwebs.

You can use all kinds of supplies to decorate your locker. Check out this list, and add some decoration ideas of your own!

What would you like your own locker's thrilling theme to be, and how will you decorate it?

★ mirror
★ sparkly streamers
★ black lace
★ plaid fabric or paper
★ photos of your ghoulfriends
★ posters of your favorite stars, like Catty Noir or Veronica Von Vamp

★ _____
★ _____
★ _____
★ _____
★ _____
★ _____
★ _____
★ _____
★ _____

A BRAND-NEW DAY AT
MONSTER HIGH

Every day at Monster High is packed with voltageous surprises. Find out what happens to me one day by filling in the blanks in my story below. Ask everyone else for words to fill in the blanks, then read the story. See how sparky (or silly) it turns out!

Totally VOLTAGE

Frankie Stein opened her coffin locker to get her [_____ noun].
She couldn't wait to get to [_____ school subject] class so she could show Draculaura her new [_____ color] [_____ noun]. But when she got to the corner, she found that the hall was blocked by a pile of [_____ plural noun].

"Oh no!" Frankie said. "These are scary-cute, but I'm going to be late for class!"

"Did I hear somebody say 'late'?" Robecca asked, [_____ -ing verb] up in her rocket boots. "You can hitch a ride with me! It'll be the cat's [_____ item of clothing]!"

"Thanks, Robecca!" Frankie said. "All these [_____ adjective] things are in the way."

"We'll [_____ verb] around them," Robecca replied. "Don't worry!"

Robecca flew Frankie over the obstacle in the hall.

"That was fun!" Frankie said. "Thanks!"

"No problem!" Robecca answered, then zoomed off [_____ adverb].

Before Frankie could head to class, she heard a(n) [_____]
animal
laughing. Looking up, she saw that it was reading one of Ghoulia's
[_____] comic books. And that made her laugh.
book title

"Why do I hear laughing?" Miss Sue Nami boomed, appearing
suddenly out of thin [_____]. "You should be in class!"
noun

"I'm sorry!" Frankie said [_____]. "I'm going now!"
adverb

Frankie scurried away so [_____] that her
adverb
[_____] flew off and landed in front of Jackson Jekyll,
body part
who was just coming out of the boys' bathroom. Frankie turned
[_____] with embarrassment.
color

"Hey, Frankie," Jackson said, but then some [_____]
adjective
music started playing, and he turned into Holt Hyde.

"Franken-fine!" Holt said. "I've gotta dash to class, but
I'll catch you on the flip!"

After Holt took off, Frankie [_____] stitched herself back
adverb
together, and a few minutes later, she slipped into her seat in class.

"Draculaura!" she whispered. "Look at my new [_____]!"
noun

WE ARE MONSTERS ✉ ✉ ✉

parts of screech ✏

Noun: a person (Slo Mo), place (Monster High), or thing (glasses)

Plural noun: more than one person (ghoulfriends), place (countries), or thing (hamburgers)

Verb: an action (write)

Adjective: describes a noun (claw-some)

Adverb: describes a verb, an adjective, or another adverb; often ends in -ly (quickly)

STUDY HOWL

gearing up for questions

Take a break to rejuvenate between classes, and challenge your ghoulfriends to see who can last the longest without making any statements—questions only! No matter how much fun you're having, don't get too geared up with excitement to remember you're supposed to be interrogatory. This game can be played out loud or in writing.

Carry on a real conversation if you want, like this one between Venus and me:

"Hey, Robecca, how was your day?"

"Do you even have to ask, Venus?"

"You got all steamed up again, didn't you?"

and so on.

Whichever ghoul makes a statement first loses the game. How long can you make it? Can you set a world record?

MONSTER HIGH

Be Yourself Unique a Monster

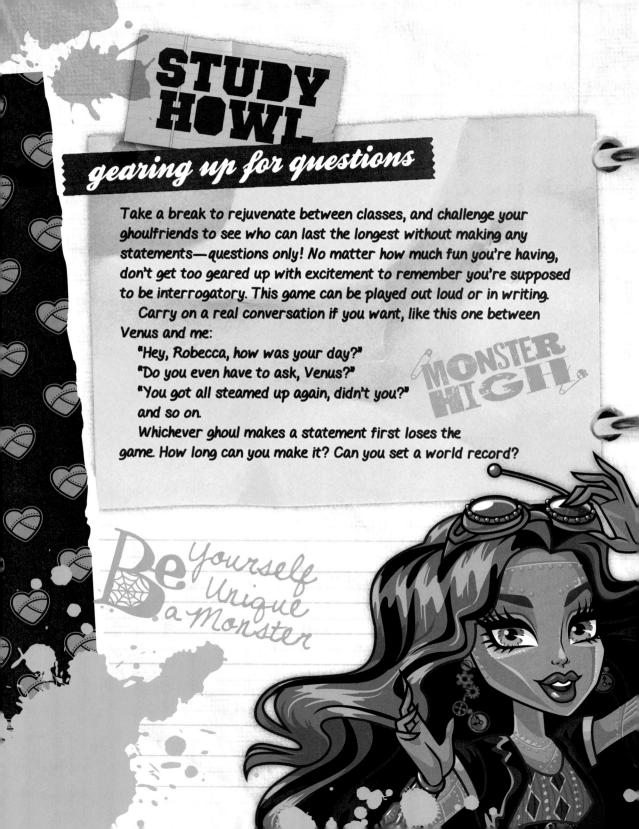

skele-skinny scarves

When you're in Home Ick class, it is so simple to make muy bonita gifts for your ghoulfriends, familia, or even your favorite teachers, to show your appreciation.

You'll need:

★ 1 skein (ball) of yarn (at least 72 yards)
★ scissors
★ measuring tape or ruler
★ a ghoulfriend to help you

Instructions:

1. Pick out some freaky-fab yarn that speaks to your style. Any store with a craft department will have yarns in all kinds of textures—woolly, furry, feathered, metallic—and every creeperific color you can imagine. Dios mio, it's so hard to pick just one!

2. Cut twenty-four strands of yarn, each nine feet long.

3. Gather the strands with the ends lined up evenly, and tie them in a knot about one foot from the end.

4. While holding the knot, smooth out the yarn and divide it into three sections of eight strands each.

5. Braid the sections together—not too loose, not too tight.

6. When you have about a foot of yarn left, tie that end in a knot too.

7. Y aquí, you have a linda scarf!

Experiment with other styles of skele-skinny scarves! You can make each section of the braid a different color, make mini-braids and braid those together, and more. Draw your own designs here!

UG-HHH-MAZING.

FREAKY FAB

alphafright soup

While you're waiting for Mad Science class to start, or after you've finished all your Dragonomics homework, give your brain a mini workout!

In Alphafright Soup, you make up a silly conversation as you go along. Start with the suggestion of a word. Any word! It could be *dragon, casketdilla, fangtastic*—whatever comes to mind. Using the word to inspire you, start writing! Each ghoul writes one sentence at a time. Each sentence has to start with a word beginning with the next letter of the alphafright.

For hexample, Ghoul 1 suggests the word *pirate*. The game might go like this:

Ghoul 2: Ahoy there, Captain!

Ghoul 3: Best be looking for land, McCoy.

Ghoul 4: Can't we all just talk to our parrots?

Ghoul 1: Diabolical birds, parrots, aren't they, McCoy?

Ghoul 2: Except for my Poltergeist Pete, who's an angel.

and so on.

See how long you can keep it going! For the letter X, remember the words *xylophone* and *X-ray*. And for Z, don't forget about *zinnias, zoinks,* and *zephyr.*

CLAWsome!

chic chef

Don't tell anyone, but cooking in Home Ick is my favorite part of school. My mom has scales and scales of recipes, and I love trying them out—and coming up with some of my own.

Here's my recipe for mummy dogs—a great snack to have after a Casketball game.

MUMMY DOGS

Good thing I remembered to keep my shades on when I made these mummy dogs. Otherwise they'd be rock-solid! They're the perfect savory snack—check out how I made them.

Ingredients (for eight ghouls):

★ 8 hot dogs
★ 8-oz tube crescent roll dough
★ 1 teaspoon mustard

Instructions:

1. With a rolling pin, roll out your dough into one square.
2. Ask an adult to preheat the oven to 375°F.
3. Grease a cookie sheet, then wash your hands.
4. With an adult's help, cut the dough into one-inch strips (for gauze).
5. Wrap gauze around each mummy dog; leave space near one end for the face.
6. Place the mummy dogs on the cookie sheet.
7. With an adult's help, bake the mummy dogs for 12 minutes, or until the tops are golden.
8. Use the mustard to add eyes in the area you left for the face.

RASPBERRY SCREAMONADE

When you're ready to cool off, try out this fresh raspberry screamonade I mixed up. Stone-cold refreshing!

Ingredients (for six ghouls):

★ ½ cup raspberries (fresh or frozen; if frozen, thaw first)
★ 4 ½ cups water
★ 1 cup fresh-squeezed lemon juice (about six lemons)
★ 1 cup superfine sugar

Instructions:

1. With an adult's help, puree the raspberries in a blender.
2. Strain through a sieve into a large pitcher.
3. Add the water, lemon juice, and sugar and stir briskly until the sugar dissolves.
4. Refrigerate and serve with ice.

CLEO'S CHOCOLATE-COVERED SCAREBERRY PYRAMIDS

When I want to give Cleo a sweet surprise, I whip up these simple chocolate-covered scareberries. (Normies call them "strawberries.") She thinks they're totally golden!

Ingredients:

★ 12 ripe scareberries
★ 1 cup milk chocolate chips

Instructions:

1. Line a cookie sheet with wax paper.
2. Wash your strawberries. With an adult's help, cut off the ends with the stems.
3. Place the chocolate chips in a microwave-safe bowl.
4. Microwave on high for 15 seconds at a time, stirring thoroughly in between. (They won't stir very well the first few times, but trust me on this. Otherwise, you might overcook the chocolate!)
5. Once the chocolate is completely melted, dip the scareberries in it one at a time. Swirl each scareberry in a circle to coat the sides completely, then shake gently to remove excess chocolate. Place on the prepared cookie sheet, flat end down.
6. Now you have a tray full of chocolate pyramids to share with your ghoulfriends! Yum!

CHEF'S SECRET: You can substitute white chocolate chips for the milk chocolate chips. If you do, try adding a few drops of food coloring to make it freaky-fab!

DON'T RUIN MY WRAP!

Mad Science

Mad Science class gives you the opportunity to make some pretty spooky-cool stuff in the lab. Help me with this final project for Mr. Hackington so I can ace this class.

slime time

Hey! Before I can get started, I need something to keep my hands busy. It helps me concentrate! Can you give me a hand with this slime?

We'll need:

- ★ ¼ cup white craft glue
- ★ ¼ cup water
- ★ red and blue food coloring
- ★ ¼ cup liquid starch (You can find this with the laundry detergent in most grocery stores.)
- ★ mixing bowl
- ★ mixing spoon

FREAKY-FAB FACT:
What's happening with the slime? The glue is a polymer, which is in strands. The starch links all the strands of glue together and makes it feel slimy.

Instructions:

1. Pour the glue into the bowl, then add the water. Stir together.
2. Add three drops each of red and blue food coloring and stir.
3. Stir in the liquid starch.
4. When the mixture is gloppy, you can start squashing it with your hands. The more you play with it, the stretchier and easier to hold it will become.

When you need to think, get out your spooky slime! When you're not using your slime, store it in a freezer bag.

Hard Rock Candy

Since Rochelle is an expert on hard rock candy—it's her fave sweet treat!—I asked her to join us to put the finishing touches on my final project.

We'll need:

★ 1 cup water
★ 2–3 cups sugar
★ red food coloring
★ wooden skewer (or clean wooden chopstick)
★ clothespin
★ tall, narrow glass
★ pot

I GOT MAD SKILLS

Instructions:

1. Hold the skewer in the glass about one inch from the bottom, clip the clothespin on the skewer, and rest the clothespin on the top of the glass so the skewer stays in place.

2. Now set the skewer aside, with the clothespin still on it.

3. With an adult's help, pour the water into a pot. Bring it to a boil.

4. Pour ¼ cup of sugar into the water. Stir until it dissolves.

5. Keep adding sugar, ¼ cup at a time, and stirring until it dissolves.

6. As you add sugar, add in the food coloring, making it fairly dark.

7. After a while, no more sugar will dissolve. It will take longer to dissolve each time. Don't give up too soon!

SO THIS CENTURY...

8. When no more sugar will dissolve, remove it from the heat. Allow to cool for at least 20 minutes.

9. Ask your adult helper to slowly fill the glass nearly to the top with your sugar mixture.

10. Put the skewer back into the glass, resting the clothespin on top and making sure the skewer isn't touching the sides of the glass.

11. When the glass is completely cool, put it in a place where no one will disturb it.

12. The crystals of your rock candy will grow over the next 3 to 7 days.

FREAKY-FAB FACT: What's happening? You added so much sugar to the water that it became a super saturated solution. The water could only hold the sugar if both were super hot. This means that when they cool, the sugar comes back out of the water and forms crystals on your skewer.

GHOULS RULE!!

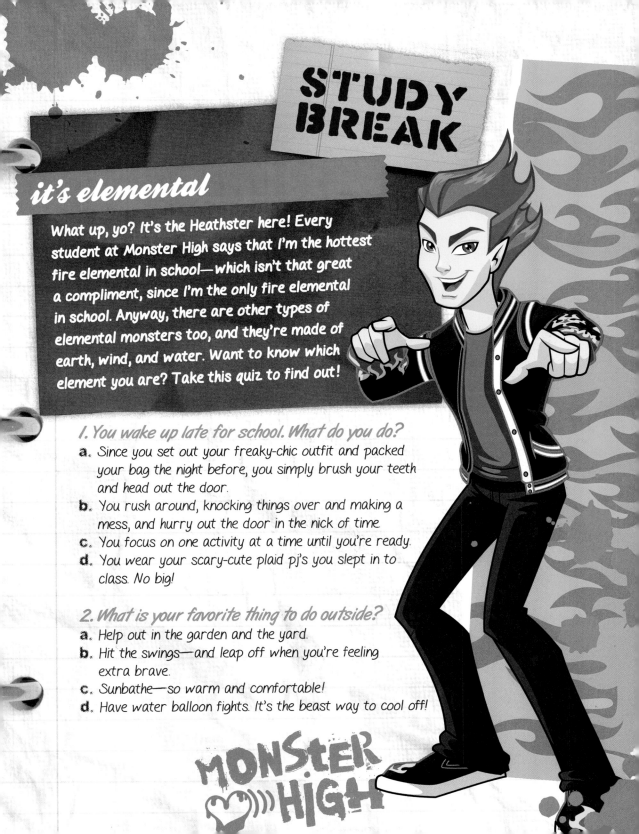

it's elemental

What up, yo? It's the Heathster here! Every student at Monster High says that I'm the hottest fire elemental in school—which isn't that great a compliment, since I'm the only fire elemental in school. Anyway, there are other types of elemental monsters too, and they're made of earth, wind, and water. Want to know which element you are? Take this quiz to find out!

1. You wake up late for school. What do you do?

a. Since you set out your freaky-chic outfit and packed your bag the night before, you simply brush your teeth and head out the door.

b. You rush around, knocking things over and making a mess, and hurry out the door in the nick of time.

c. You focus on one activity at a time until you're ready.

d. You wear your scary-cute plaid pj's you slept in to class. No big!

2. What is your favorite thing to do outside?

a. Help out in the garden and the yard.

b. Hit the swings—and leap off when you're feeling extra brave.

c. Sunbathe—so warm and comfortable!

d. Have water balloon fights. It's the beast way to cool off!

MONSTER HIGH

3. What's the beast after-school snack?
a. ghoulam crackers
b. ice-scream sandwiches
c. chips and spookalsa
d. abominapples and honey

4. You get a good grade on the big Ghoulish Literature final. How do you celebrate?
a. Read a book that *wasn't* assigned for class, like *The Haunter Games*.
b. Throw an oxygenerific party, complete with dancing.
c. Head outside to let off some steam.
d. Take a relaxing bubble bath.

5. What is your favorite sport?
a. cross-country running
b. downhill skiing
c. Casketball
d. swimming

GHOULIDS FRIENDS FOREVER

If you chose mostly **A**s, you're an Easygoing Earth! You're sensible and calm. Don't be afraid to go crazy every now and then!

If you chose mostly **B**s, you're a Wild Wind! You're always in a whirl. If you feel stressed out, take some deep breaths and do some stretches before leaping back into action.

If you chose mostly **C**s, you're a Freaky Fire. You're intense and focused. Allow yourself a break if you start to feel like you're burning at both ends.

If you chose mostly **D**s, you're a Wavy Water! You're very chill and laid-back. Don't be afraid to be feisty if the occasion calls for it!

PHYSICAL DEADUCATION

Getting your body moving really energizes your brain.

Physical Deaducation is the beast place to burn off the energy you've built up by all the hard work you do in your other classes. Make the most of it!

SCREAM TEAM

GLOOM BEACH RELAY

Some days your mind's at the beach, but your body can't get there. If today is one of those times, here's a fun race to get both mind and body in the spirit of the beach, even if you're not close to the water. Fortunately, this relay race will put you in a perfect beachy mood!

For each relay group, you'll need:
★ masking tape
★ beach chair (A folding chair works too.)
★ towel
★ sunglasses
★ copy of *Teen Scream*
★ beach bag

Instructions:

1. Divide into teams of at least three ghouls each. Use the masking tape to mark the starting and finish lines. Put the towel, sunglasses, and magazine in the beach bag.

2. When the relay starts, Ghoul A on each team races to the finish line, where she sets up the beach chair, lays out the towel, sits in the chair, puts on the sunglasses, and opens the magazine.

3. Next, Ghoul A puts everything away and races back to Start.

4. When Ghoul A gets back to Start, Ghoul B repeats steps 2 and 3.

5. The first team to have all ghouls finish the relay is the winner.

Freaky **FAB** in Every **WAY!**

CASKETBALL BAG GAME

When you're ready for fur to fly in the gym,

get your claws on the ball and shoot

some haunted hoops with your ghouls.

You'll need:
★ 5 paper grocery bags without handles
★ 3 small, soft balls
★ a piece of masking tape or some other floor marker

Instructions:

1. Place the open paper bags in a line.
2. Mark a spot on the floor three feet in front of the first bag.
3. Stand behind the mark on the floor and try to sink three shots. You get 1 point for each shot in the closest bag, 2 for the second bag, 3 for the third bag, 4 for the fourth bag, and 5 for the fifth, and farthest, bag.
4. Once every ghoul has had a turn, tally up the points. Then go for a rematch!

FEARLEADING

Without Fearleaders, there are basically no team sports, because how can you demonstrate your athletic prowess without someone to fear you on? You can't! Fearleaders are incredibly important.

To see if you've got what it takes to go to Monster Mashionals, try writing some fears of your own.

HOT TIPS:

★ Clap your hands along with your fears.
★ Every line you write should have four claps.
★ Rhyming is of the utmost importance.
★ Spelling words out is golden.
★ Repetition is good. It makes it easy for the crowd to chant along!

We R the 'IN' CROW

check out this Monster High fear:

Monsters! Monsters!

Go, team, go!

We are fighters!

It's our show!

A PYRAMID OF POM-POMS

A Fearleader without pom-poms isn't a Fearleader at all! Follow these simple instructions to make your own set.

You'll need:

★ clean, empty plastic chip bags (3—4 per pom-pom)
★ scissors
★ masking tape

Instructions:

1. Smooth out your chip bags and stack them together.
2. With an adult's help, cut off the bottoms to make all the bags the same length.
3. Cut a slit in each side of the bags to help them lie flat.
4. Cut one-inch strips lengthwise in the bags; leave about three inches at the top uncut.
5. Squeeze the uncut ends of the bags into a handle and secure with masking tape.
6. Repeat steps 1 through 5 to make your second pom-pom!

get schooled

Each new class is an opportunity to monsterfy school supplies! Use the fangtastic stickers in this book to decorate binders and folders. Punch out the bookmarks to use as creeperific placeholders when you study!